The Marathon Runner

by Jan Weeks

illustrated by Paul Harrison

PiCTURE WiNDOW BOOKS
Minneapolis, Minnesota

Editor: Jill Kalz
Page Production: Melissa Kes
Creative Director: Keith Griffin
Editorial Director: Carol Jones

First American edition published in 2006 by
Picture Window Books
5115 Excelsior Boulevard
Suite 232
Minneapolis, MN 55416
877-845-8392
www.picturewindowbooks.com

First published in Australia by
Blake Education Pty Ltd
ACN 074 266 023
Locked Bag 2022
Glebe NSW 2037
Ph: (02) 9518 4222; Fax: (02) 9518 4333
E-mail: mail@blake.com.au
www.askblake.com.au
Text copyright © 2000 Jan Weeks
Illustrations copyright © 2000 Blake Education
Illustrated by Paul Harrison

Printed in the United States of America.

Library of Congress Cataloging-in-Publication Data
Weeks, Jan.
The marathon runner / by Jan Weeks ; illustrated by Paul Harrison.
p. cm. — (Read-it! chapter books. Sports)
Summary: After months of being chased by his new school's biggest bully,
fifth-grader Sam is ready to run a marathon during an athletics competition.
ISBN 1-4048-1669-0 (hardcover)
[1. Country life—Fiction. 2. Bullies—Fiction. 3. Moving, Household—Fiction. 4.
Marathon running—Fiction. 5. Running—Fiction.] I. Harrison, Paul, 1972– ill. II. Title.
III. Series.
PZ7.W4216Mar 2006
[Fic]—dc22   2005027162

Table of Contents

Chapter 1

Beacon Hill Is Cold

Saturday, March 18

Dear Felix,

I told you I would write, but you didn't think I would, did you? Anyway, there's not much else to do at Beacon Hill. It's cold all the time, so I stay inside a lot.

When I do go outside, I think my ears and nose are going to freeze and fall off. I wonder how I would look with no ears or nose. Like an alien maybe?

I wish we hadn't moved. I wish we still lived near the city. If only Peter's asthma wasn't so bad. You and I could still play soccer and go to the movies on Saturday afternoons.

7

Peter likes it here on the farm. I knew he would. Uncle Serge thinks he's wonderful. He calls him Buddy. He calls me a little pest. He says I should stop being so grumpy.

I hope Mom and Dad come soon. I miss them.
How long can it take to sell a house?

Your friend, Sam

Chapter 2

Milking the Cows

Sunday, March 19

Dear Felix,

Uncle Serge just drove us into town. That's where we're going to live when Mom and Dad come. He showed me the bank where Dad is going to work. I think I might like it better living in town than living on the farm.

Uncle Serge expects us to help with the milking.
I can hear the cows now, slowly walking up to the
milking shed. Did you know they had to be milked
twice a day?

I don't like cows. I really don't. Yesterday, one stepped on my toe. There's no way I'm going to be a dairy farmer when I grow up. I don't even like milk—not since I found out where it comes from. I'd rather have a glass of water.

Peter says he's going to be a dairy farmer when he grows up. I guess that's why Uncle Serge likes him so much.

E-mail me soon!

Your friend, Sam

Chapter 3

School

Friday, March 31

Dear Felix,

It's me again! I started school this week. I was hoping Uncle Serge would forget about it, but he didn't. I'm still in fourth grade, but the school is much smaller. There's only one fourth-grade class here.

Peter and I ride the school bus. It stops right by the front gate of the farm. I think it's way too far to walk to school, but my uncle says we should try it. He says he had to walk farther to get to school when he was a boy. I nearly asked him if he had to watch out for dinosaurs, too! Ha!

My teacher's name is Mrs. Hill. She seems OK.

I have to go. The cows need milking again!

Your friend, Sam

Chapter 4

▣ Fishing and Owen Turner

Sunday, April 2

Dear Felix,

Uncle Serge took us fishing yesterday. He showed us how to catch trout. It's called fly fishing, and it's really fun. Uncle Serge caught three fish and fried them for us for supper.

Today, I went to the river by myself. On the way back, I met a big, tough kid with curly hair named Owen Turner. He jumped out of the bushes and landed right in front of me. I almost jumped out of my skin!

"Hey, kid, what are you doing on our land?" he growled, grabbing my arm and twisting it behind my back.

"I didn't know it was your land," I said.

"Well, you'd better keep out," he roared, "or you'll be sorry!"

Then he let me go.

When I was far enough away, I stopped and yelled back at him, "You're not so tough! If you were, you'd pick on someone your own size— a gorilla maybe!" Then I flapped my arms and made chicken noises.

He chased me all the way back to Uncle Serge's house. He yelled at me to stop so that he could hit me. As if I'm that stupid!

Peter said that he'd heard Owen Turner was the meanest kid in school. He said I had better stay away from him. I wish I'd known that sooner!

Your friend, Sam

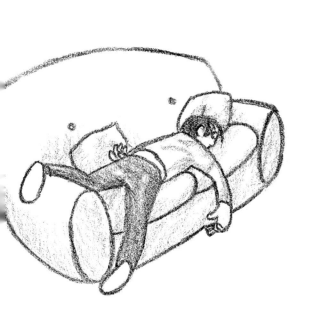

Chapter 5

Owen Turner's River

Saturday, April 15

Dear Felix,

Mom and Dad came to stay for the weekend. They think they might have found someone to buy the house. Peter hasn't had any asthma attacks here, so Mom and Dad think they're doing the right thing by leaving the city.

Guess what? I caught my first trout! It was so exciting. I could see it in the water before I pulled it out. At first, I thought it was silver, but then I saw all of the other colors. This kind of trout is called a rainbow trout. Fishing is the best thing I've ever done.

I just wish I didn't have to fish in Owen Turner's river. Right after I caught the trout, Owen saw me and started chasing me. I dropped the fish and was too scared to go back and pick it up. Now Peter doesn't even believe I caught anything.

Owen has chased me four times now. He keeps saying he's going to slug me. Yesterday, I finally thought it was going to happen. Owen and a couple of his friends had me cornered in the playground. I was lucky a teacher came by and saved me. Phew!

Your friend, Sam

Chapter 6

Thursday, April 20

Dear Felix,

The principal said we are going to have a track and field day two weeks from today. There will be running races, a high jump, a long jump, discus throwing, a tug of war, relays, and a marathon.

Peter is happy. He's good at sports and won most of his races last year. Remember? I've never won a race in my life.

Bye for now!

Your friend, Sam

P.S. I don't know what a marathon race is. Do you?

Chapter 7

Catching Fish

Friday, April 21

Dear Felix,

Uncle Serge is helping Peter train for the track events. I could train, too, but I get all the exercise I need running away from Owen.

I fooled Owen yesterday! I got up really early to go fishing. I caught three big fish, and this time I got to keep them.

At first, Uncle Serge wasn't too happy that I didn't help with the morning milking. Then, he saw the fish.

"Wow!" he said. "Three fish! Well done! We'll have them for supper tonight."

Oh, and I found out what a marathon is. It's a long-distance running race—26 miles, 385 yards (42.2 kilometers) to be exact. Mrs. Hill said that it's the last event in the Olympic Games. You need to be in really good shape to run such a long distance.

Our marathon will go up to the top of Beacon Hill, along the track past Owen's house, and then down the main road back to school. It's a long way.

I just hope I finish. Uncle Serge said he'd buy me my own fishing rod if I do.

Write when you can!

Your friend, Sam

P.S. Mom called last night. She said she saw you at the grocery store with your folks.

Chapter 8

Track and Field Day

Thursday, May 4

Dear Felix,

We had our track and field day today. Peter won nearly all of his races. Uncle Serge says Peter's long legs were made for running.

I came in second in my heat. My teacher said it was a good effort. Uncle Serge said the same thing. I came last in the final, though, because I tripped at the beginning of the race.

When it was time for the marathon, it started to rain. It rained so hard that the marathon was postponed until next week.

I wasn't sad. Owen said he would slug me during the marathon. He found out that I hid his backpack in the girls' bathroom.

See you!

Your friend, Sam

Chapter 9

Marathon Day

Thursday, May 11

Dear Felix,

We finally had our marathon race today. We all lined up by the school gate. There were about 90 of us competing.

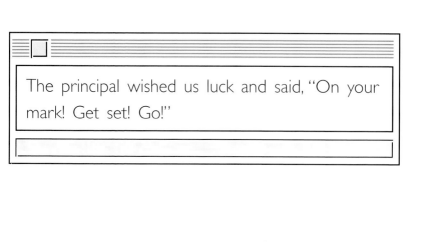

The principal wished us luck and said, "On your mark! Get set! Go!"

We were off, running through town, getting ready to charge up Beacon Hill.

People stood on the streets and cheered us on. It was like we were at the Olympics!

Peter was ahead of me. So was Owen. I thought if I stayed behind him, I'd be all right.

The long run up Beacon Hill was hard, but I kept on going.

Uncle Serge was handing out water to the runners as they ran by.

"The leaders aren't too far ahead of you, Sam," he said. "Keep going and you might catch up."

We had been told that if we got too tired, it was OK to stop running and walk. A lot of the other kids were already walking, but I kept on running. I wasn't really tired, and I wanted to finish the race.

I was running along the track near Owen's house when I saw him. He was hiding behind a tree, waiting for me. It was too late for me to avoid him.

"Got you!" he said as he stretched out his big arms and dragged me behind a tree. He was getting ready to slug me. His fist was in the air, and he looked pretty angry.

I don't know what made me think of it, but I yelled, "Look! There's your dad!" and he let me go.

Then, like a shot, I was off! I was really, really racing. My legs were going faster than the rest of me.

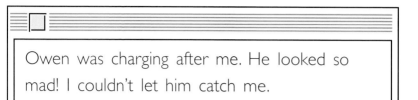

Owen was charging after me. He looked so mad! I couldn't let him catch me.

I sped out onto the main road. I kept passing other runners until there was only Peter left in front of me. On and on I ran. My legs were hurting. My lungs were hurting. But I couldn't stop—not with Owen behind me.

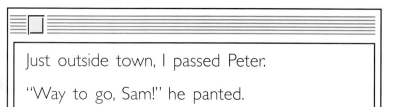

Just outside town, I passed Peter.

"Way to go, Sam!" he panted.

Into town I ran, along the streets and through the school gates. I felt better and better with each stride. A minute later, I was the winner of the marathon!

Everyone crowded around. They all cheered and clapped. The principal congratulated me on my great run.

I was hot, I was sweating, and I could hardly breathe, but it didn't matter. I felt like a giant. I felt like a hero!

Owen came in second place, and Peter came in third. Everyone made a fuss over Owen, too. He even shook my hand. Then his mom made him put his arm around me so she could take a photo of the winners.

Mrs. Hill said I show great promise. She even said that one day I might be asked to run in the Olympic Games.

I don't care about running in the Olympics. All I really want to do is go fishing in Owen Turner's river. Maybe now he'll let me. He knows he'll never catch me!

I'll e-mail you again soon.

Your friend, Sam

Glossary

avoid—to keep away from

congratulated—praised warmly

cornered—where one cannot get away

dairy farmer—a person who keeps cows to milk

milking—getting the milk from the cow

principal—the head of the school

promise—good things to come

Technical Terms

athlete—someone who is trained in a physical activity

discus—an event in which a heavy, circular metal plate is thrown

final—a race in which the heat winners run again for first, second, and third places

heat—one round or division of a race

long distance—races of more than .5 miles (800 meters)

marathon—a long-distance running race that's 26 miles, 385 yards (42.2 km) long

track event—a running race

tug of war—two teams pulling on opposite ends of a rope

Marathon Course

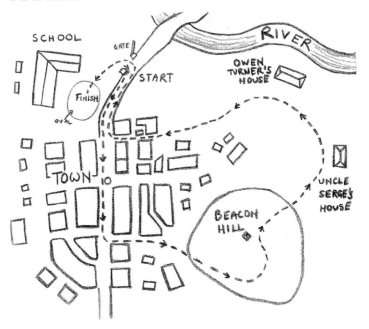

Equipment

LOTS OF WATER

T-SHIRT

SHORTS

RUNNING SHOES

Basic Rules

- A marathon is run for a distance of 26 miles, 385 yards (42.2 km).

- Men and women run the same distance.

- Marathons usually start early in the morning, to avoid the heat of the day.

- There must be a drink station every 3 miles (5 km).

- Any number of people can participate.

- There are rules about the course. It cannot be too hilly.

Training Tips

Warming Up and Cooling Down

- Before running or jogging, always warm up.

- Stretch your arms and legs.

- Go for a brisk (fast) walk to warm your body. After running, cool down by walking and stretching.

Style

- Try to jog/run at an even pace when training.

- Your goal when training for a marathon is to build fitness and endurance, not speed.

Stamina

- Run on all surfaces—rough and smooth. Practice running up and down hills.
- Have a running partner to encourage you.
- Don't push yourself too hard. Don't run too fast, or you won't make it to the end. Pace yourself.
- Each training session, increase distance bit by bit.
- Rest days are essential to give your body a break.
- Cycling and swimming are excellent activities for days when you are not running.
- Enter as many races as you can. This will help you gain experience among crowds of people.

Look for More
Read-it!
Chapter Books

Dash! Crash! Splash! 1-4048-1662-3

Home Team 1-4048-1667-4

Horsing Around 1-4048-1666-6

Let Toby Lane Play Goalie 1-4048-1662-2

The Super Electrics 1-4048-1663-1

Tennis Balls and Rotten Shrimp 1-4048-1664-X

Tomorrow's Olympian 1-4048-1665-8

Looking for a specific title?
A complete list of *Read-it!* Chapter Books
is available on our Web site:

www.picturewindowbooks.com